THE BIGGEST PUDDLE IN THE WORLD

Written by
MARK LEE

Illustrated by
NATHALIE DION

Groundwood Books
House of Anansi Press
Toronto   Berkeley

Charlie and I were staying with Granny B. and my grandfather Big T. for six whole days.

The first day,

we explored all the rooms
in the big old house.

THE BOOK
OF
MAPS

Then it started to rain.

So the second day, we stayed inside
and explored a few more places.
But it kept raining.

The third day, we played dress-up.
And the rain didn't stop.

Charlie and I wanted to go outside, but
there was too much rain!

Big fat drops of it splattered on the
ground. Water gushed out of a gutter spout.

"Where does the rain come from?" I asked my grandfather.

"I'll show you when the storm passes," he said. "But first we'll have to find the biggest puddle in the world."

The biggest puddle in the world! How big would that be?

The next morning, patches of sunlight appeared on the kitchen floor.

"Big T. is outside with Keeper," Granny B. said. "After breakfast, you can go exploring."

Charlie and I found Big T. chopping wood.
"We want to find the biggest puddle in the world," I said.

Big T. put down his ax. "Then let's go look for it."

The wet earth and the shiny grass smelled like spring. During the rain, a clump of mushrooms had popped up on a fallen log.

"There's a puddle," I said …
… and Keeper jumped in it!
"It's not a very big puddle," Charlie said.
"I guess we'll have to keep searching,"
Big T. said.

Wild flowers had opened after the rain. Bees
crawled inside them like little balls of buzz.
Keeper found a puddle beneath a willow tree …

... and Charlie and I jumped in it together!

"That was still a small puddle," I said. "We
need to find one *bigger* than that."
Our grandfather smiled. "Follow the water."
Charlie and I found a trickle coming from
the puddle.

And that combined with other trickles and fed into a stream.

We followed the stream and it emptied into a pond. Water striders glided across the surface. In the shallows, tadpoles emerged from filmy white eggs.

"The pond is like a big puddle."

"That's right. A lot of small puddles make a
bigger one."

Big T. scooped up some water with his hand
and dripped it onto a flat rock. Then he pulled out
a pencil and a piece of paper and
asked me to draw a
puddle map.

When I was done with my map, I looked at the flat rock. The water had disappeared!

"Where did it go?" I asked.

"Look up and you'll see. The water in the air becomes the clouds in the sky."

"This little pond makes all those big clouds?"

"It's water from ponds and rivers and the biggest puddle in the world."

I jumped up. "Let's go find it!"

On the other side of the pond, we found
a river. We followed it through thorn bushes
and down a muddy hill to a beach that faced
the ocean — the biggest puddle in the world!

The cold wind smelled like slippery seaweed.
Waves rolled in with a rushing, hushing sound.
 Charlie touched my arm. "You're it!" he shouted.
 And we ran along the edge of the surf, kicking
up spray.

Back at the house, we took off our wet
clothes and ate dinner at the big table.
Granny B. served blackberry pie with
ice cream for dessert.

That night a new storm arrived. Raindrops rattled on the roof and trickled down the window panes.

And I was happy because the rain and the puddles and the pond and the ocean and Charlie and Keeper and my grandparents were all connected to me in a wonderful way.

"Charlie ..." I whispered. "Do you hear the rain?" But he was already dreaming.

For Kirsten, Lili and Helen: three
people who love big puddles.
M.L.

To my mother, who has been an
inspiration since always.
N.D.

Text copyright © 2019 by Mark Lee
Illustrations copyright © 2019 by Nathalie Dion
Published in Canada and the USA in 2019 by Groundwood Books

Groundwood Books / House of Anansi Press
groundwoodbooks.com

We gratefully acknowledge for their financial support of our publishing
program the Canada Council for the Arts, the Ontario Arts Council and the
Government of Canada.

Canada Council   Conseil des Arts
for the Arts   du Canada

ONTARIO ARTS COUNCIL
CONSEIL DES ARTS DE L'ONTARIO
an Ontario government agency
un organisme du gouvernement de l'Ontario

With the participation of the Government of Canada
Avec la participation du gouvernement du Canada   Canadä

FSC
MIX
Paper from
responsible sources
FSC® C012700
www.fsc.org

Library and Archives Canada Cataloguing in Publication
Lee, Mark, author
The biggest puddle in the world / Mark Lee; illustrated by Nathalie Dion.
Issued in print and electronic formats.
ISBN 978-1-55498-979-9 (hardcover). — ISBN 978-1-55498-980-5 (PDF)
I. Dion, Nathalie, illustrator II. Title.
PZ7.L439Bi 2019   j813'.6   C2018-902611-1
C2018-902612-X

The illustrations are a mix of real and digital watercolors.
Design by Michael Solomon
Printed and bound in Malaysia

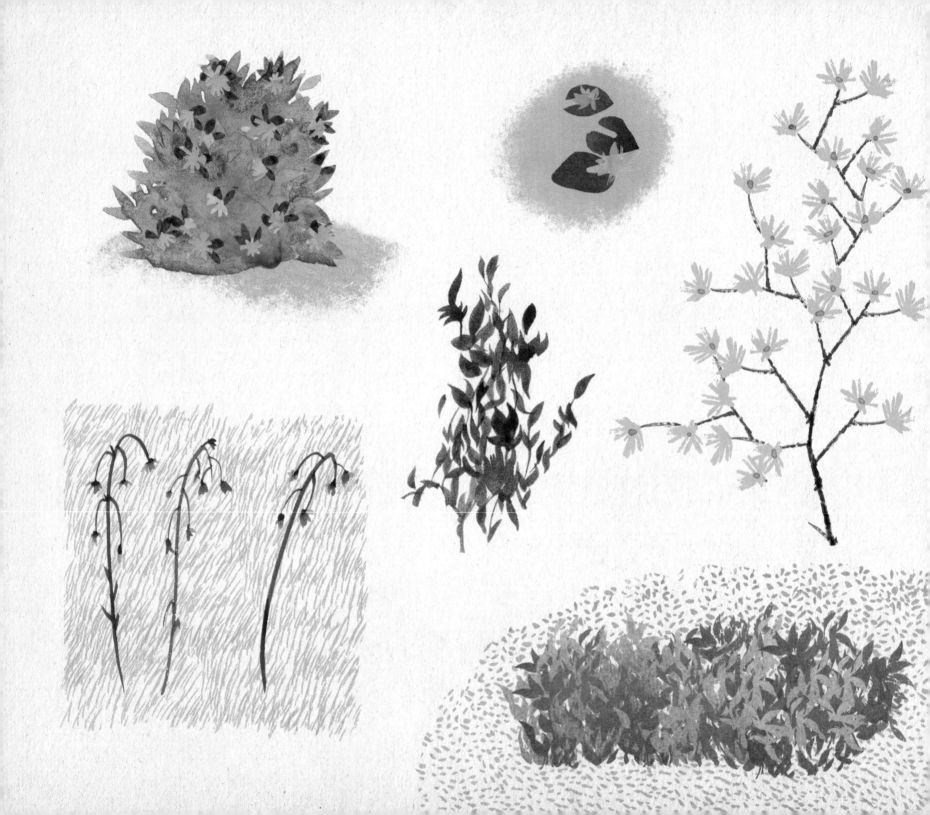